Learning
To Swim

Learning
To Swim

Marjorie Saiser

STEPHEN F. AUSTIN STATE UNIVERSITY PRESS

IBSN: 978-1-62288-211-3

For more information:
Stephen F. Austin State University Press
P.O. Box 13007 SFA Station
Nacogdoches, Texas 75962
sfapress@sfasu.edu
www.sfasu.edu/sfapress
936-468-1078

Distributed by Texas A&M Consortorium
www.tamupress.com
Book Design: Ben Adams

Contents

III. Through the Thin Wall

I. Close to the Shore

Happy

Not the way my aunt fixed my hair
that morning, not the length
she rolled and pinned
against the back of my head

not the way my to-be in-law
said what she said,
not the way my for-better-or-worse
didn't intend to stick up for me

not the sounds my shoes made
under my long white dress
their clipped syllables on the stairs
up from the church basement.

This was when I was sailing close
to the shore of my life.
That boat capsized, thank my
lucky stars, and since then

I've been bobbing in the deep,
splashing, coughing,
water in my throat at times,
learning to swim.

And Do We Need to Go Down Too?

Is it all right to stay afloat
when asked to drown, when
someone reaches to pull down?
This is a great mystery. I won't
solve it. I won't solve it by drowning.
Our grandmothers gave their lives
and I should honor that. I won't
honor that by drowning.
They tell me to honor that
by drowning. Those are my/
our instructions. Here's a
log to float on. I won't
honor it by drowning. Here,
sing this song with me,
this song about not drowning.

Word Gets Out About the Divorce

Word gets out and my neighbor Rudy
comes across the yard to say Good for you!
and Rudy's dark-haired wife, petting the head of
their golden retriever, says Come over Friday night
Come over for munchies. Word gets out and
I think I'm guilty of looking like someone
with a get-out-of-jail-free card. Before their father
arrives to pick up the kids for the weekend,
I take them to the ice cream store.
We stand in front of the array of choices
making up our minds, my daughter
with her third grade split-decision ponytail
coming out of its holder, my son wearing his
eleven year old I-can-take-it bravery
and in this moment I see I have done it.
I have for better or worse cast our lots.
Cherry Chocolate Happiness or Jamaica Almond Regret.
Who knows? But it seems like today is a good day for
the three of us to have double dips
and for good measure sprinkle on a few of those
little imported chocolate candies.
I think they're called Don't Look Backs.

Axis

I was pregnant, no amount of lying
could fix that the night I told my parents I was
getting married. It was dark and late,
dark and late having led me into trouble
and now I walked my thickening body
into my parents' unlit bedroom,
the window a dim rectangle,
my mother not saying a word
from her side of the bed,
my father flat on his hard-working back,
staying calm as I have also learned to do
when people let me down.
"Any reason you are getting married now?"
His question hung below the ceiling.
My chance to own up.
"No, no reason," I lied.
The baby wasn't wrong, tadpole
upside down in a pocket within me.
The question wasn't wrong; it was a porch
I could have stepped onto
and turned around to face the road.
My mother wasn't wrong either,
choosing silence in the dark.
Who was wrong?
Not even the young woman I was,
standing wet-faced
before turning as if on an axis
to take her body, her child, her upright spine
to her own room and her own narrow bed.

Girl in the Stucco House

Maybe I can outlive
the sad girl in the stucco house.
I intend to get as close
as a girl from sadness can

to that red star which hung
south of town on summer nights.
It's a long trek, a narrow ledge I fall
from often but I'm getting up

this morning as my old teacher
taught me and I'm heading off,
the latest insult stuffed deep inside
my backpack along with my self-

inflicted leg irons. My feet are healed
a little, my common idiom like
manna in my mouth, my one good
eye trained on distance.

Cocktail Party

I turn away from the person who is
lecturing me on what he has
accomplished, who does not ask about
my life, though I have one.
It would be, I suppose, polite to go on
nodding to this success who thinks of me as
a listening post, and not so long ago
I would have stayed, listening,
but the runway is short,
the engines revving,
the sky limitless and I begin to know
the expanse I am stepping into.
I begin to see it will be empty
and lonely and quiet and peaceful
and I will not be shoulder to shoulder
with what I did and made and perfected
but will rather suspend
and be suspended
and, in slow motion,
turn and turn again.

Occupations of the Body

The tunnels of the body fill and empty,
the larynx, when it has no lines to say,
waits silently in the throat,

and the membranes
of the small drums also wait.
The muscles of the heart,

the circles of its valves
know their opening and closing
so well. The chambers of the body,

its fringes, its fronds,
the hidden white sticks of its bones,
its cells with their boundaries

fit together, almost ecstasy,
sending out into the world
the least lash or hair.

My

Often in my mind I replay it:
that moment when the fox

slipped along the edge of my yard.
My yard, I say. *My*. But I see

how it is. It's his grass,
his tree trunk, his row of shrubs,

no line he may not cross, his path of brick,
his patch of woodchips. The canopy

is his and I am an eye,
like the bird's eye. I'm surplus

birdsong. The silent fox slips
yard to yard in the city, curls up,

his nose covered with the brush of his tail,
to wait out the time of noise and light.

Every Last Thing Is Transitory

Today again the cardinal
hopped about on the grass,
red against green. Today again
he flew to the lilac bush
and went into it. Some day
everything will be eaten up
or sunk into a space even darker
than the tar at Le Brea. Still,
this morning I vacuumed the floors
which will be gone, I shook rugs,
I unwrapped a new bar of soap.
I am not ready. My daughter,
that creature I love. Not ready
for any goodbye. Her hair,
which I love, supple and dark.
And her hands suddenly still from their
knitting, from counting the stitches
around the circular needle,
her fingers lifting a strand of yarn
and pulling gently to make a little slack
for working. You may have noticed
I am not ready to let go.
The summer we went to the lake.
The day we moved our baggage
from the car to the cabin. I want
that day, all that baggage,
and her feet up the wooden steps,
her arms carrying her baby. I will
not give that. We are slated to
disappear like a red bird into
green foliage. There has never
been anything else, just this
everlasting leaving.

Plastic Bag on the Lawn

I was staring into the dark
because I couldn't sleep and then the wind

blew an empty white trash bag
along the ground in the yard. The plastic

moved like a woman
writhing in grief, rolling,

reaching out her arms,
crawling forward,

her head barely rising
then slumping. I stood at the window

and watched what I knew
to be lifeless. I knew what it was

and what it wasn't. It fooled the dog
too. So I knelt beside him

and told him it was okay, listened
to the growling in his throat,

listened to the air
around the shell of the house. Just enough

moonlight to keep the grass dark
and the ghost white. Her legs

caught on the stalk of a rosebush.
She filled and emptied and filled with sorrow.

One Winter in the Desert

I had a bed in a room with a glass
door I pulled back to step out and
look at the stars. They were cold
and large, the stars, clinging to black
as if they knew their places:
the big dipper upside down over the roof,
Orion over the silhouettes of palm trees,
Cassiopeia in the north, her skirts
washed out by the faint glow of Tucson.
I'd go back in, sliding the door
shut on the cold and sparkle,
then into bed again, my familiar quilts,
my dog, my book. It was more warmth
and beauty than I deserved, more wealth.
When daylight arrived with its generous colors,
I walked down to the arroyo and entered there,
got to know which bird was talking to me,
maybe the cardinal clicking in the cholla,
maybe the curved bill thrasher's high note,
or a hummer buzzing in the mesquite,
and sometimes, with luck, the gray hawk
making its noiseless exit from a branch,
opening its wings for a long glide, unflapping,
leaving me looking up, showing me
what I never did master: a swift straight line
when you know exactly where you are going.

I Save My Love

I save my love for what is close,
for the dog's eyes, the depths of brown
when I take a wet cloth to them
to remove the gunk. I save my love
for the smell of coffee at the Mill,
the roasted near-burn of it, especially
the remnant that stays later
in the fibers of my coat. I save my love
for what stays. The white puff
my breath makes when I stand
at night on my doorstep.
That mist doesn't last, gone
like your car turning the corner,
you at the wheel, waving.
Your hand a quick tremble in a
brief illumination. Palm and fingers.
Your face toward me. You had
turned on the overhead light so I would
see you for an instant, see you waving,
see you gone.

When Wind Blows All Day

When wind flutters the neighborhood palm trees,
when it fingers the leaves of oleanders

and pins down the low-lying laurel,
when it rattles the flapper of a vent on the roof

or finds some corner to moan against,
then I'm back on the plains with snow

in the air, snow which will all day
brush against the shingles. A heavy woman

in a cotton dress opens the maw of a coal stove
and drops in a chunk of what's left of her winter supply.

She shuffles in cracked shoes to her kitchen
and will do her best to find something to fill me.

I Walk in My House Among Stacks of Papers

Useless things I've saved. My nest much too large
so I fill it, make a small space for myself.

Flotsam, jetsam, books, shoes,
plastic totes along the stairs,

mounds of clothing, a dead fern.
I want to go easily as everyone else

seems to do; I want to turn left on Esperanza,
park in any available space, lock my car

without triple-checking, walk the trail.
I want to feel my wings open at the shoulders

like any sparrow and, like any sparrow,
drop into unwalled air.

If I Had Wings at My Shoulders

I would keep them folded
loving as I do
to walk on sand or grass
to breathe in the world's fragrances
kiss its sweethearts
but I've been stung
by its jealous bees, I've seen
the curve and rush of its armored scorpions
I've cried alone in its caves
been seen as catchable
a warm body
without recourse.
There was the day the cat of my death
placed one paw down then another
stepped quick and hungry along the woodchips.
I fluttered out of her claw
I knew I was lucky
when I lifted myself,
my beating heart in its slender case,
shingles to wire to branch
any branch.
I left her on a patch of ground,
left her staring, slit-eyed, tail twitching,
she with four earthbound stubs,
she who must always
touch something.
I left her, small as a pebble,
below.

Edith Porath Nelsen, You Signed Your Quilt

You embroidered your name
in a corner in blue thread after you
sewed these squares together.
You hemmed your quilt, you folded,
you laid it into storage. It came to me,
no blood relation. Edith, I know your name
and your diligence, round and round,
eight stitches to each inch that lies
over my knees. Sometimes, Edith,
I pull your quilt up around my chin and
sit in the yard under constellations.
I listen to silence, I make plans,
as you may have made plans. I save things
I'll never use. I use irreplaceable minutes,
hours. Dark squares from a gray shirt,
squares of rowdy blue flowers. I'll have to
wash this, Edith. It will go into water and suds.
I'm trying to see patterns. Stars I've been told
are belts and swords; I'm trying to see how
it's me, broken stitched to broken.
They tell me to shut up, shut down,
the ever-present *they*, as maybe they told you
and you told others. Edith, I want to keep
going a few more thousand rounds,
to use what I've been given, what came to me,
to squander it in the best way I can,
I want to make it matter.

Useless Sleep, What Map or Friend

What map or friend I have there
does not come over the sill.
No memento. A percentage of my
years unconscious

and only dreams report.
I've been breathing deep,
acting and acted upon, but why?
I want to know what it is

I do and feel
when I am traveling
so far abroad.
How did that tune

go? It was some syllables
I can't repeat.
Some medium my more
solid self can't swim in.

Start Up

Get the heat going under the kettle
early while it's still dark,

ready a cup and a tea bag,
wait, standing

alone in the kitchen before the day begins.
This is my work, this is my life,

to tip the kettle and pour
and then to see an ant, floating in the cup,

one of the little ones who have sometimes
lately come running out from a stack of papers

on the counter, suspended now,
a small dot hanging

in the ocean of my tea. There's morning light
in the window panes, there's

birdsong beginning.
What a strange thing living is,

this breathing. There is not enough of it,
the inhale/exhale my friend used to do

on a day like this one, some bird
with no touchable home, taking hold

of a high twig, all the town below,
all this air for free, to make song of.

Looking Around in the Galaxy

Here I am again, alone,
the neighborhood quiet,

constellations flung above me. Tonight
Cassiopeia doesn't look much like a monarch.

I need a new picture. Maybe a scribe,
wheeling on a very large scale. I recline

on my chaise lounge, my dog in my lap,
my fingers in his fur,

all this turning slowly
toward a point not yet visible,

once in a while an airplane blinking
a path from right to left through stars.

Beyond my stone wall
four or five crickets are noisy in the weeds

like all my old enemies—what was it
I had against them anyway?—I forget.

Weren't We Beautiful

growing into ourselves
earnest and funny we were
some kind of alien, smiling
the light we lived in was gorgeous
we looked up and into the camera
the ordinary things we did with our hands
or how we turned and walked
or looked back we lifted the child
spooned food into his mouth
the camera held it, stayed it
there we are in our lives as if
we had all time
as if we would stand in that room
and wear that shirt those glasses
as if that light
without end
would shine on us
and from us.

II. Facing the Dog

After the Divorce the Soccer Game

I went to my son's soccer game
he wasn't crazy about soccer but he
always did what he was signed up for
it was a cold day and I had his jacket
but he refused I held that windbreaker
for most of the game it kept its place over my arm
it was a cold day and some of the other kids
were wearing jackets but he wouldn't
he looked cold blue-lipped and his upper arm
was cold when I broke the ancient
iron-clad rule to lay my hand on it
I didn't say a word because at least I knew
some of the rules but I had taken the easy way
the divorce I wanted my son to be warm
waiting to return to battle waiting for the coach
to send him back to run and to fight
and to do the noble thing
which his eyes told me I had not
he shook his head not even the full gesture
just half a head shake only what the game allowed
just half but enough No coat mom never any coat.

Facing the Dog

The dog is the size of a pony, his muzzle waist high. He gives eye contact, always eye contact, his tail the size and length of my arm, raised, oscillating like a needle on a dial, paws and haunches large even for his large body, standing his ground on the graveled street, a tawny coat, black jowls and ears, continual deep-throated barking, challenging us since he appeared suddenly and began to follow our family group as we were talking and walking along in the middle of the street of the little town, there being no sidewalks.

My son, Paul, is carrying our rain ponchos and carrying a long rolled up umbrella, also carrying years of experience with challenges. He steps toward the dog, says loudly: "Go home. Go. Home." This tactic, I know, works for many dogs but not this one.

No one comes from the houses along the street, not one townsperson emerges to call off the dog. We are the outsiders. Earlier, at lunchtime, I was face to face with a man in a cowboy hat ready to step out of the cafe just as I was ready to step in. In this situation, one thing that often happens is a smile and a pleasantry. I looked up, anticipating a smile to match mine. His face was stony. No flicker of acknowledgement of another human being; it seemed to me more of a stare. I felt my own reaction rising within my body. I had disdain too. I looked on him as foolish, full of bluster, silly. So this is what happens: we take sides, we do not meet as equals, I refuse to cower, be less than, and so does he.

But back to the dog in the street, and my son standing before it. An old story: the family goes into the cave and one stands without, facing the teeth of the beast. Where is god? In the sinews of the father's legs, in his arm, in the stick of the umbrella at the ready? Is god in the houses, their windows to the street but no one opening a door? The disinterested bystander? Is god in the beast, growling? I do not have answers. The man in the cowboy hat striding to his pickup has answers. And so, in a way, does my son. He faces the dog,

32

the dog barks, spit drooling, the minutes tick by in the standoff.

My son has brought his family to this, my hometown, to view the local museum. He wants his boys, Josh, 9, and Reuben, 5, to see where their grandmother grew up. He has asked me to travel to meet them here for this foray into family history. There isn't much left of the town except the museum, housed in the old clapboard Catholic church. We've had lunch at the cafe, one of the few businesses still going. The keeper of the museum, Ann, has driven her truck into town from her ranch to meet us at the museum with the key.

Ann is waiting at the church; we can see her standing beside her truck. We had decided to walk from the cafe to the church, and now we have the dog challenging us, barking, his big paws following our every step if we move. If we stop and turn to him, he growls. He takes another step toward our family, bays to the sky. Paul's five-year-old is hanging onto his daddy's leg. Paul tells both his sons to go to their mother and stay at her side. I know it is good for all of us to stay in a close little knot. Paul tells us to walk to the church/museum. My husband, Don, decides to stay with Paul and the dog. The rest of us, sometimes backing, make our way together down the block away from the dog to the open door of the building.

I stand in the door with my grandsons and we watch the men and the dog. Let me remember my feelings, my impressions. The dog is indeed a danger, but the children are safe. It is my job to keep the children inside the cave and to be calm, let them see this drama. It is my son's job to face the dog, stand his ground as the dog stands his.

The boys refuse to stay inside the cave but they do stay near the opening and so do I. We stand as if we are caught in amber or are stick figures in a cave drawing. "Ann," I say, "maybe you could get into your truck and go pick up the men."

She agrees, fishing her keys out of her pocket , saying, "I was thinking that. Thank you for putting it into words." I can tell it is the thing she wants to do. What holds us back sometimes?

The houses with their empty eyes?

Ann's truck goes rolling toward the men and the dog. The

barking continues, deep and rhythmic and rasping. The vehicle slows; perhaps Ann is saying something to the men. She drives beyond them and makes a U-turn in the intersection, comes back. Don gets in. Paul does not.

The truck comes back and pulls up again at the church. Paul walks the distance to us, lagging behind the truck. I hear the steady steps of his sandals on the gravel. The dog stays where it is. It's as if the spell has been broken. When Paul gets close to the church, the spell is so broken that the five-year-old runs to him, leaps a puddle, shouting: "Daddy, you're alive! you're alive."

A Word After a Word After a Word

My neighbor James shows up for a moment in his kitchen window as his light comes on and goes off. I'm lying on a couch on my porch in the dark and James is turning from his sink to his table. He appears for a quick blip and is gone. A tree trunk covers most of the window, the tree having gotten wider and covering more in the years we've been neighbors.

When you can't sleep and you are thinking in the dark, as I was, your mind can turn to remnants of memory. I'm thinking of my sixth grade teacher, Mrs. Fischer, at the chalkboard showing us how a sentence looks if you diagram it. One of the most useful and beautiful things I learned from her: a system of lines hanging off the base line of a subject and a verb. I think of that system every once in a while. I'm thinking of it now as I write this sentence, how adjectives hang off the nouns, how words relate to other words, how thank would be the verb in the sentence I'd shape for Mrs. Fischer in that architecture she taught me. People who love tapestry might like to turn over a wall-hanging to look closely at the backside of it. That is the way diagramming is for me: a way to appreciate how language is put together.

Mrs. Fischer loved language and knew what its power was, so she drew its shadows on the chalkboard. It's possible that of those who sat in her classroom, I'm the only one who uses diagramming. Not that I regularly sketch out a sentence, but anytime I want, I can be aware of subjects and verbs holding court with their nobles around them. Which doesn't mean I never use a fragment. I do. But I recognize it as a fragment, a chunk off the main block.

I'm remembering how my son Paul, his wife Julie, and their boys made a long trip to visit my hometown and the cemetery. The plan: to lay pebbles on the headstones of our forebears. Paul had invited me to be there, and I, too, had made a long drive in order to take part in the pebble laying.

Standing in the cemetery, we can see the town in the distance; hayfields are all around us. The meadowlarks sing, one here, one there, hidden in the shortgrass prairie, their flute-like notes pouring back and forth over the graves, as I had told the boys they would. Weeks before, when we had stood in their kitchen in Missouri, the family had clustered around my phone to hear the meadowlark's song on an Audubon app.

"That's what you'll hear at Grandpa Louie's grave," I had said. "You'll hear the larks." I had choked up then and hadn't got to the rest of a long paragraph, and so the boys were spared. It surprised me that my throat closed and my eyes teared. Just the recorded song of a meadowlark. Just a subject and a verb about a grave.

We certainly hear larks as the boys choose stones from their stash and place them at various markers, this smooth pebble for a great grandfather they never knew, this pointy granite chip for a great grandmother a couple of tiers up from their own names on a family tree I sketched for them. I place pebbles, too, including one at the headstone of my mother's father, who had abused me. I hadn't previously thought of his grave, but of course there stands his headstone with the others. I say nothing and place a pebble close to his name, planning to give all this a lot of thought later. When my husband, walking around among the gravestones, had read that name aloud, I could have ignored it completely. I didn't.

In his path among the headstones, my husband had also said the name of Mrs. Fischer. Until then, I hadn't known the location of her grave, hadn't known the year of her death.

Louis Leonard side by side with Marjorie Lucy. Louis John with Anna Marie. Forebears the boys do not know. But in previous weeks in their walks at home, they had collected pebbles for this little ceremony. Not a formal ritual at all, rather just conversation about which stone they are choosing out of the handful, and where they will place it, the boys lively over the grass and around the headstones, the grown-ups moving easily too, but more slowly.

We finish up and return to our cars for the next thing on our list: lunch. But then later I'm wishing I had laid a pebble on the gravestone of Mrs. Fischer. It's one of those actions, those homages, which make no real difference in the world. No one needs to know, but you do the modest ritual to complete something in yourself. So later, in crisscrossing the county that day in our two cars, I tell my son that I will stop briefly again at the cemetery to lay one more pebble. "I forgot my teacher," I tell him.

When my car pulls off the highway to make this second stop at the cemetery, our son also stops his car. I expect everyone to wait in the car, but they get out and come to the grave to see me place my pebble.

My son says, "We were talking just now, asking Josh who his favorite teacher is, and we wondered what made Mrs. Fischer special to you." Behind my sunglasses I'm teary and my throat is in the grip of an iron hand. I'm sure to sob if I try to answer. I try. I get out a few words: "Mrs. Fischer had the amazing ability to . . . "

If, as Margaret Atwood says, a word after a word after a word is power, my power had hit a road block. Think of those people who break down in public, people who want to say something close to the heart, something they need to put into language but when they have the moment to say the important thing, they cry. I imagine the brain has the sentences but it's the throat that can't manage or it's the heart, that great mystery, which fills with feeling and becomes so full the words can't get past the vocal cords. How disappointing to freeze up, the face contorted, tears welling, while words stay in limbo. The person waves off, gives up trying to say.

Not wanting the grandchildren to be puzzled by my crying and by the awkward silence of the grown-ups, I choose to let my tribute—I don't know exactly what it would have been—go mostly unsaid. I manage to get one word through the roadblock. I keep composure behind my sunglasses, and perhaps it wasn't such a bad tribute. Truncated, but summing up at least one of the qualities I was grateful Mrs. Fischer had. I say my sentence and the family receives it, perhaps knowing it is all I can manage and that it stands for much

I cannot at this point say. I finish my sentence, "Mrs. Fischer had . . curiosity."

I'm glad at least that word made it through the barrier. Curiosity: the quality of thinking you don't know it all, that there might always be new things to figure out, that surely the world will always be worth discovering, leaf by leaf, person by person. Not with didains or superiority but rather with a sense of appreciation.

It was her generosity I wanted to convey, how in a town off the beaten track she could impart appreciation for a larger world while respecting the spot where she was. For instance, she taught standard usage: "You'll need to know the correct verb tense *see, saw, have seen.* You'll need that for your travels in universities but don't go correcting your elders at the supper table when they say *have saw.* Your elders know what they need to know and can teach you so much." She had no false sense of superiority. The important thing was respect.

She showed up in my life, one very lucky thing for me. Years later, when I was back in town and had a few minutes of conversation with her at a gathering, I had an opening for a sentence to her about how important she had been to me. It wasn't a well-constructed paragraph but a few words that tried to get at something immense, not an oration, not a boulder but a pebble placed in great respect. And that day she received my sentence, didn't dismiss it or refute it, but listened to it with composure, and then came the usual interruptions and the great swirl of the dance, but it had been an opportunity to say the gratitude I felt.

A simple pebble laid in a simple way. Not a grandiose speech, rather a subject, *I,* and a predicate that couldn't do everything but did a little toward describing feeling, one human to another. Each of us doing what we do, and perhaps without knowing it, being that momentary rectangle of light in the dark.

Just a glimpse, a blip. We stand illuminated for a minute, being ourselves, being real. and then the light is gone again.

Two Pictures

When our family group walked the streets of my hometown, I felt unwelcome, not only because of the dog, but also because of a Confederate flag flying at a house we passed. The children didn't notice, or at least they didn't comment on the flag. They were talking about the blossoms they picked from a hedge near the street, the bushes heavy with small red trumpets, the boys trying to make the trumpets pop when smashed into the palm, as I had described I had done as a child. Nobody mentioned the flag and we walked on.

What message did I take? I saw the flag as a warning, its message to me: you are not welcome here; you must think of America in a certain way or you must leave. That flag broke into my happiness. But in that same town Ann waited for us at a door. She welcomed heartily, generously. The staring eyes of the houses, the Confederate flag on its pole, the aggressive dog hounding us. But also Ann. One picture and the other. Both exist in my world. I will pay attention. It's not that I want to ignore the Confederate flag warning, but I don't want it to blot out the other picture.

Pass It On

When Reuben shouted "Dad, you're alive, you're alive!" it broke the silence. It made those of us in the church/museum laugh; it ended the drama. My daughter-in-law, Julie, putting the best construction on the event, said the dog's owner must be unaware that the dog was loose. I disagreed, saying that if you choose to own a powerful animal, it is your responsibility to know where it is. Behind its windows, the town said nothing. I didn't see from which yard the dog had emerged. I didn't watch where it had gone away. The road was empty when I thought to check after the general rejoicing.

We went into the the museum/church and walked up and down looking at photos and old stoves and meat grinders and coffee cannisters and newspapers. But I was thinking of the herd of cattle which had long ago run toward me, a four-year-old, in an open pasture.

Horns. Staring eyes. They faced me and charged, stopping of course before they reached me. My grandfather could easily have picked me up and carried me instead of leaving me, barefoot, running after him, crying, picking my way through the prickly pear. The cattle wouldn't charge a man in overalls and a felt hat, but they weren't used to small screaming child. They reacted to me. Him they ignored. I didn't ignore their bulk, their nostrils, the curve of their horns, their lowered heads, either that day or in the nightmares that followed. I could have used a grown-up who could see things from my perspective and could give me some calm.

Contrast my son's actions with my grandfather's walking away to leave me alone with the beasts. True, I did survive, as he figured I would. The cattle didn't gore me; they scared me, which he thought was foolish and laughable. Contrast his non-protection with his descendant's behavior. Perhaps my son had a model he was following as he faced the dog. Maybe the model is in books. *The Lord of the Rings*, perhaps, and/or some other story my son read and loved. My grandfather was not into fiction. He trusted his own experience and the market reports. I never saw him read anything except the county newspaper. He listened to, and I had to shut up for, the ringside announcer during blow-by-blow boxing matches on the radio. His daughter, my mother, read to me in my early years and I am grateful for wherever that urge or that wisdom came from.

She Told Me to Spread My Wings

The town lies on short grass prairie north of the highway, exactly where it lay when it was the known world to me. I lived on Main Street then, in two rooms attached to the back of Midge and Louie's Cafe. Either Midge or Louie was at the grill, frying hamburgers until 10:00 p.m., which my teacher, Mrs. Fischer, would have called putting in a good day's work. Which is what you have to do if you are the only cafe in town and you are trying to scratch out a living turning burgers, or standing behind the counter, serving slices of the pies Midge made during the afternoon lull.

Midge, my mother, could make good pie crust, pinching the edges with her big fingers, making pastry fit the circle of her glass pie pan. She called it making "shells," and she filled the shells sometimes with raisin cream and sometimes with thick hot lemon pudding, which she had stirred in a pan we called the granite pan. It wasn't granite. We called a lot of things what they weren't.

Those who turned south off the highway found themselves on Main Street, two blocks long. And they would have seen a concrete block building on the west side of the street, just where my father drove four stakes and laid out the dimensions with blue string when he got back from the Philippines and WWII. (Mrs. Fischer called that doing your duty.) He laid the blocks course on course, the walls rose, and he left two large rectangles on the front for two plate glass windows.

I stood often at those windows. What I saw was the east side of Main Street, including Trauernicht's Cafe, Schmitz's cream station, and the White Horse Bar. I said Midge and Louie's was the only cafe in town, but that's just something we said; there was Trauernicht's Cafe too, run by my friend Beverly's mom. A friendly rivalry. Beverly was older and probably not a good influence. (Mrs. Fischer's phrase was *slippery slope*.) Beverly told me to steal cigarettes from the bar behind the counter of our cafe. The bar was not a bar, it was a piece of furniture against the wall, varnished wood, triangular peak, and there packs of Camels and Winstons stacked up, to be bought by the smokers in town or dutifully stolen by me, age 10, and given to Beverly, age 12, who could just as well have stolen them from her own mother's cafe. I got sick from smoking and of course the secret came out, along with the contents of my stomach. (Mrs. Fischer, if she had known, would have called it throwing up one's toenails.) I confessed to my mother that I'd been smoking and I begged, between heaves, that she would not tell my father or Aunt Emma.

Even retching, I noticed my mother's smile and wondered about it. I know now there was no way she would have told Aunt Emma, and she smiled to think I would think she might. She had her strong likes and dislikes. Emma, my father's childless righteous red-headed aunt, fell on the dislike side. My mother also did not admire Mrs. Fischer, but I did.

My mother's dislike reached way back to her high school days: something about a white dress with a red sash. All the girls in my mother's class were to sew a white dress from the same pattern. Everyone arrived in the required dotted Swiss, but one girl had added a very red, very wide sash. When I looked at Mrs. Fischer at the front of our classroom, yes, I could see her with swash-buckling scarlet around her waist.

Both my mother and Mrs. Fischer were strong women with dark hair and glasses, my mother in flat shoes and blue jeans, Mrs. Fischer always in dresses and wedgies. I admired Mrs. Fischer because, as gossip said, she had left the county and the state, had married and divorced. When she came back to our completely white-bread town, she brought her child, a girl with brown skin. She married again, a rancher. I heard a cheeky sixth-grader at recess ask her why she came back. She answered, "Because I fell in love." It was the way she said it, as though it were the most simple riddle in the world.

Mrs. Fischer told me to take both my regular spelling test and also the sixth-grade test, and to lay the extra test on her desk without fuss; she'd correct it and give it back. Use everything you've got, she told me, no matter what anybody else says. After school on that first double-test day, Mike Krajl told me if I wasn't careful, he would slap my snot-nose show-off face. He did shove me around and push me off the sidewalk, but I survived.

There was the morning Mrs. Fischer brought into our classroom a woman from Algeria. I had never seen black skin for real and now when I went to the map to point out Algeria and its capital, I was within touching distance of this beautiful woman, her incredible teeth, her dress of many colors. I noticed how she had applied her magenta lipstick inside her natural lip line. Instead of math that day, we found out about her travels and what was different about our town and hers. The world is a big place, Mrs. Fischer said, and it's fun to find out things.

I liked the way Mrs. Fischer took her pitch pipe out of her desk drawer, blew a note on it, said "This is *do*. Our song begins on *sol*. Sing down to *sol*." I liked the way she sang "Rose, Rose, My Rose of San Antone." I liked the way she talked about Evangeline, searching for her lost love. I liked how she recited "The moon was a ghostly galleon tossed upon cloudy seas; the road was a ribbon of moonlight over the purple moor." There was so much to like about Mrs. Fischer.

My mother should have been a teacher. She loved algebra. Many afternoons after school, some high school student would spread an algebra text and papers on the counter in the cafe, beside a bottle of Coke and a bag of Planters peanuts, and my mother would lean over the counter to explain equations. She'd give her sermonette about how beautiful algebra is. She'd practically take the student's hand and lead them into the pristine waters of binomials. My mother loved explaining how to find x.

I suppose my mother did tell my father about my smoking. He was a quiet man and I imagine he said little about it. He would not have punished me; he never did. It was just that I didn't want to disappoint him, let him down. I did let him down mightily in my twenties, but that's another story. In this part of the story, I was doing all right.

Once in a blue moon I make that turn off the highway onto the gravel of Main Street. I don't shoot through town and on out, as most travelers do, but pull up and park in front of the current cafe, which is located where the old post office used to be and which, the sign tells me, is actually the Town Bar and Grill. Midge and Louie's cafe is boarded up, and the picture windows are not looking out on anything. My mother had known every customer who came in, or at least knew their folks and where they lived in the county.

This town was an excellent place to grow up and the Saturday night dances were one of the reasons. If you were ten years old, you and one or two of your cohorts could slide around on the dance floor between dances, run halfway the length of the hall and then slide the other half, because some member of the band had sprinkled corn meal on the boards to make things more dance-able. You could get in one or two good slides before a grown-up told you to quit it and go home. If Mrs. Fischer were in attendance, you didn't slide at all but minded what she called your p's and q's.

If you were in your teens, you would not slide, but dance. Hot sweaty summer nights with the doors propped open and the three-man band playing polkas and waltzes. If you were the daughter who lived in the back of Midge and Louie's Cafe, you would walk at intermission from the dancehall to the cafe to help serve hamburgers and pie to the dance crowd. A lot of the dancers didn't make it to the cafe but stopped off at the bar.

Sometimes there were fights at the dance. Two guys with raised fists and bloody noses, one woman trying to stop it. A couple of townspeople would stop it, or at least push the fight outside the dancehall. The fight would continue for a while in the alley.

Today I sit at a table in the new cafe, where the waitress doesn't know me and couldn't care less. (Mrs. Fischer would call that not knowing me from Adam.) I'm eating my French fries, and I'm thinking that before I drive to the cemetery with my two wreaths in the trunk, I'll swing by the empty schoolhouse, drive once around the block, a sort of tribute to Mrs. Fischer (she might have called it giving credit where credit's due). Mrs. Fischer, whose every assignment, every red mark, every circled B+ at the top of my paper, got me ready to get back on the highway.

What She Taught Me

She taught me linking verbs, predicate nouns,
long division, have a Kleenex ready, an apple
a day. She taught me three-quarter time, Greenwich

Mean Time. She taught me *do re mi*, Mexicali Rose,
Rose, Rose, my Rose of San Antone. She taught me
Peas Peas Peas Peas, Eating Goober Peas.
She taught me that a peanut is a goober pea

in certain parts of the world, that it is fine
for things to be different in different parts
of the world, no two goobers alike in their

dry red skins, their pock-marked pods,
that there are latitudes and longitudes we have
never seen, that she had seen some part,
and so would I, that I need not

forego either hopscotch or baseball, that spelling
is on Friday and it is OK to learn more
than one list, including the hard list; it is not

showing off—it is using what you have.
That using what you have will not please
everybody, that marrying a man of a different stripe

is not a popular thing in a small town world,
and divorcing and coming home with a child
is even worse, and that you
get up every morning anyway,
and do your work.

Brome Grass is Tall Around My Mother's House

So much is gone. Glint of glass
in the window where she watched the road.
White paint on the columns of her porch.
She would have mowed that brome,
would have laid those seed heads down,
she'd have kept the yard in her fashion.
The house sags. The pear trees
have persevered but they tilt,
and some branches
have the odd angle of broken arms,
yet the brome grass celebrates,
waving like a crowd. Jubilation
of wind, as if cheering for her.
Come, shy lady, take a bow.

This Year I Did Not

make the trip to lay flowers
on your grave, no real excuse,
and somehow I hope you won't be

mad. It's as if you're still alive
and I must please you. None of this
is your fault, the pleasing. I can't

make the drive, my reasons
flimsy as curtains billowing
in a spring wind but I loved you

then and now, you of exquisite excuses,
and so I stand in my imagination
in a prairie cemetery where

a bird, unseen, delivers
this morning a complex song, quick notes,
flute-like. Again. No audience but

the plain unadorned grass.
I think you understand.
A bird on the ground

singing, even when refusing
to show herself.

This is the Photo of My Father Before

he went to war and came home,
before he built a cafe in his small town,
breaking that stunted street open to
hamburgers and French fries and bean soup,
back from military housing and mess halls
to drop down into sepia on paper
and become what he has been ever since:
thin shoulders under a blue shirt,
coffee with cream,
duty with fresh bread, chokecherry jelly,
finish before dark, stay at it
until the last nail is hammered,
stay at it, last log on the pile
sawed and thrown onto the wagon,
last cow milked and headed out the barn door.
But listen, I am tired
of pails of grain and loyalty,
tired of a thousand times when he
washed cups and plates in soapy water
in the kitchen after closing, tired
of each heavy cup following another
and his big fingers handling dishes.
What I loved, I mean,
was that tree, that real thing,
that hackberry he was.
Strength and rough bark,
roots lengthening down into dry loam.
I live my life here in the city
every day, but when I want,
I can think about mountains, how they
rise from the plains through clouds.
Unseen, undeleted, steady.

I Pretend I Can Remember

It is springtime in Texas when
I am conceived. There is much

sunshine though I can't know sunshine,
cocooned as I am. Sunshine

and puddles of orange flowers
on both sides of all the roads.

Oh how these two love!
The apartment would burst its seams

if they loved one more iota. Unhappy
is what the years will bring

but I don't know that yet,
upside down, growing, getting my nails,

my eyelashes.
Sound of a drum, steady,

and always a noise
like rushing water.

Outside, but very close, he lays his hand or his head
(he is warm and foolish—I will love him)

where she tells him to lay it.

The One With Violets in Her Lap

the one with violets in her lap
— Sappho

is my mother, young, sitting
cross-legged on the grass, my mother
before she tired,
her unbitten hands in her lap, their only job
to hold the flowers or to smooth
her dress over her knees. In a moment
she will be old. A small wind
moves the hem of her skirt.
She sees you coming now across the grass.
Something good happens in her eyes and she
lifts one beautiful cream-colored arm to wave.

For the Record

She was happy and then not happy
and she didn't know how to get it back.
Neither of them knew how to get it back.

Skinny legs long arms dark hair blowing
and no smile.
It had been a good smile

as when something unties, unbinds, lets free.
That's what it was like, though there is no record of it.
Let me be the record of it.

He Taught Me to Drive

The road wasn't a proper road; it was
two ruts across a pasture and down
into a dry creek bed and up

the other side, a cow path really,
soft sand up to the hub caps.
You didn't gun it at the right time,

he said. I knew that before he
said it, but I didn't know how to get
the old Chevrolet out of the crevice

I had wedged it into. *You'll figure it out,*
he said, and then he took a walk,
left me to my own devices, which until

that moment had been mostly tears.
My face remained nearly dry,
as was the gas tank when he finally

returned, took a shovel out of the trunk,
and moved enough sand from around
the rear tires so he could rock

back and forth and get a little traction.
That country had very little traction;
it had mourning doves, which lay their eggs

on the ground, a few twigs for a nest,
no fluff. Mourning dove. Even the name
sounds soft. Even the notes they coo,

perched on a fence wire. But they are
hatched on the dirt. When they leave the shell,
the wind is already blowing their feathers dry.

Ruby T

My first grade teacher, Ruby Tienken, was a character; *character* was the word I heard in my hometown for the old woman with the jaunty step. We didn't use the word *eccentric*. *Character* implied she had a strong will and was out of the ordinary in her attitude. Ruby didn't keep her head down.

Even as a barefoot preschooler sent down to Martin's grocery for a loaf of bread, I recognized Ruby was not the usual. The way she dressed, the way she stepped along the aisles gathering her canned goods into the one cart that Martin's grocery had. Ruby T in a two-piece dress, almost a suit. Most women, including Mrs. Martin at the checkout counter totaling up Ruby's purchases, wore dresses they'd sewn themselves. Or like my mother, they wore jeans and a blouse from the Sears catalogue.

Ruby wore black lace-up heels. I saw a similar pair recently in the window of a specialty store for dance shoes. "Retro peep-toe." Yes, I'm sure she could have danced in those.

She strode where others would tread softly on the oiled boards of the grocery. Ruby made an entrance, a presence, but not because of her size. She was petite and lively. She was old and sprightly. Old was a word often appended to her. Old Ruby Tienken. She didn't drive. Her son, Henry Newton Tienken, waited in the driver's seat outside the grocery. Ruby strode to the Olds with her sack, got into the back seat, and Henry Newton chauffeured her home to her mansion overlooking the river.

In my teen years, I once spent a few minutes in the living room of the mansion. My father had some business to discuss, and Ruby came out to our car and graciously invited us in. Dad turned down her offer of lemonade. While they did some paperwork, I looked around the room. What the townspeople called the mansion was a large house, more like a hunting lodge, with stuffed heads of deer on the walls, dark framed oil paintings of a river and trees, a landscape I'd seen all my life, but this helped me see oaks and elms and hills in a frame I'd not had before, seeing them as art, especially the art of the river, the glimpse of it mostly obscured by greenery as if in a Jane Austen novel.

Ruby's living room smelled of ashes and wood smoke. I wasn't used to that. Our house was heated by propane; a large blimp-like propane tank sat in our backyard, similar blimps in the yards of my friends. But Ruby T had a fireplace. The romance of it! Soot around the bricks, and gray ash here and there on the hearth. The first fireplace I'd seen, except in my mind as I read Nancy Drew books at my family's yellow Formica table after the supper dishes were done and put away.

Ruby T seemed to be out of a book, with her long hair pinned up at the back of her head. Everybody else's hair was bobbed like my mother's and permed every few months with a Toni. A Toni came in a box, a kit, with pink plastic rods about the size of chicken wing bones. You rolled wisps of your hair around the chicken bone and fastened it close to your scalp. You covered your entire head with the chicken bones. Your friend or relative squeezed Solution A from its plastic squeeze bottle onto each bone while you sat on a kitchen chair with your face in a towel to keep from inhaling too many fumes. You set the timer. Solution B was the neutralizer. When the timer dinged, you hung your head over the sink (the towel was really necessary then) while your friend or relative squeezed Solution B over each hair-wrapped rod. The rods were removed and immediately you had the newly permed look, until it wore off in a month or so; then you had the between-perms look, ready for your next Toni.

But Ruby T did not hang over a sink for her hairdo. Maybe she didn't have a friend to do the neutralizing. More likely, she didn't want the look everybody else had. She wound her long hair into a kind of crown and fastened it up with a tortoise comb, the comb having more history, I suppose, than most women in the county could scrape together, certainly more than came out of a Toni box purchased at Martin's Store.

Ruby's hair may have been red in her youth but it was gray when I saw her striding around town. I don't mean to give the impression she was imperious. She was quite approachable. She strode because she was purposeful. She was not snooty, she was lively, and a small town cannot forgive that. Besides, she didn't go to church, so the town said she put on airs and thought she was better than. Maybe that's the cardinal sin: *better than.* There were regular people, the nucleus, and then on the periphery circling in an orbit, there was the character, Ruby T. She didn't sew her own clothes, she didn't Toni, and she strode. Three strikes and you're out. The town did tolerate her and let her buy her canned peaches and have her fireplace above the river. They labeled her a character and let her be.

I was ready to go to school and, lucky creature that I am, the first grade teacher that year was Ruby T. I've been lucky all my life, and here's an early instance. When Ruby T told the school board she would teach first grade, I was, though I didn't know it then, launched into my own orbit, circling literacy and hanging on to a large chunk of wonder.

One of my classmates was Roger. Roger held his book upside down to read *Run, Spot, run.* I'm sure Roger knew his book was upside down, Spot running on his head. All the kids in the circle knew Roger's book was upside down. And Mrs. T knew Roger's book was upside down.

Roger was older than the rest of us first graders, and he was smaller. Perhaps malnutrition was part of that, and certainly heredity. He may also have inherited (and maybe this was nurtured at his house) a certain kind of rebellion. Roger, diminutive, had a large capacity for the passive/aggressive. Sweet little Roger of the big eyes over the top of his inverted blue primer.

When it was his turn to read in the circle, Roger recited from memory what he knew went with that picture. He wasn't going to learn to read if he could help it. Mrs. T got up from her chair in the circle and click-clicked in her heels over to Roger, turned his book right side up, and asked him (so reasonably) to read it again, please. If he wasn't going to learn to read, that was his choice, but there were rules to this game.

At my turn, I knew *See Spot run* by heart also, but I was making the connection between the runes on the page and the sounds coming out of my mouth. I loved it! Power! I could not have articulated it at that age, but it was definitely power. Deciphering of code.

Mrs. T didn't stick solely to the blue primer. She also played a reading game with us and in this game, I got to run in the classroom if, on the chalkboard, she printed my name followed by the word *run*. Not even Roger could resist this. It was not a full-out run as from third base to home plate on the playground, but it beat sitting at a desk.

I said even Roger had to decode, but he didn't, because the rest of us could read *"Roger, run."* So when Mrs. T wrote it on the chalkboard, our eyes turned to Roger. He didn't read the chalkboard; he read our faces. Who's to say this skill wasn't more useful in his life? He stood up and ran around the perimeter of the room in the prescribed course. If the words on the chalkboard actually said *"Roger, walk"* or *"Roger, skip"* he had fun anyway. And he had a 33 1/3 % chance of guessing right. Mrs. T chose her battles and taught the decoding of English to those of us who were ready, and she spoke respectfully to those of us for whom decoding groups of odd marks was not yet useful.

To the Author I'm Reading at Night
— for Sharon Olds

Because of the way words
sound in the room when I am
sitting up in bed, reading,
I read aloud your tribute to your
elementary teacher, how she saved you,
and knowing that someone somehow
saved *her*,
and someone saved *her*
and so on up the ladder,
not tribute exactly, more than that
and my voice takes a timbre,
a quality from solitude.
I feel I could
understand my mother, how she
loved in a crooked sparkly foolish
deep way and I have that in me too,
my time in the cone of light, my dog
on the end of the bed licking his paw
and knowing nothing, like me,
of hate circling the planet, I'm
forgetting it on purpose and enjoying
this yellow lamplight because someone,
your compassionate teacher, saved you
and you pass it on, black letters in a string,
string after string, to me,
someone alone in a chamber, noise of
traffic outside the walls,
nothing but night in the window,
someone you don't know, reaching
for the rope of that connection.

III. Through the Thin Wall

Possum on the Patio

She shouldn't be scary, but her hands
look like human hands that haven't
been in the sun for a long time, troubling

because of the way they tremble. She
settles into a gait that takes her along the edge
of the yard and under a row of leafless bushes,

her body a color that perhaps a shape-shifter
might be, her eyes black holes, long-nailed fingers
white like the moon, fluttering as if she's

considering whether to cross the yard at all.
Twitching. For some reason you are calling it
she. You shiver. She speeds up and

before she vanishes, looks back
as if she's seeing her fate,
or you are seeing yours.

What Was Surprising Was Not

that they sang. I had heard larks
before, but this was different
because all night it had rained,

off and on, sometimes soft, sometimes
drumming the roof. What was
surprising was that before sunrise,

before the night was over,
while the trees were yet dripping,
the larks sang to one another.

One east of the house, the other south.
I listened from my perch
at a window in the second story.

They tossed their song in the dark,
weightless, back and forth.
They began their work without light.

What Love Is

Love is on the road to pick you up,
as hoped. Headed in your direction,

the gas tank full enough
and the day spilling over

like sun on the road.
It's possible.

Or maybe love is
the green chrysalis of a monarch butterfly,

ready to be a remarkable
new thing. Just now the future dangles

by a slender thread under the eaves.
It's almost time, it's cramped in there,

you can see its fresh colors
showing through the thin wall of the case;

it's very nearly ready to step out
and flutter its new wings dry.

I Didn't Think I Would

I didn't think I would, you weren't
exactly my type, it was your clean
short fingernails, your Adam's apple
when you were trying to say
what you weren't used to saying,
and then how you liked to go
out to breakfast, omelets and toast
and lots of coffee, it was how clean
and waxed your floors were, cold
and hard and dustless and you so
warm in your shirt, so showered
and shaved, careful colors
and I would strew clothing
on your floors and pile books
on those flat bare surfaces,
set cups with a click on a dresser
or a sink or a counter. I wasn't
trying for anything, it was—
it *is*—just a spell I want to be under.

Non-Listener

I explain how I escaped,
how the blizzard tried to stop us,
but my listener is walking away.
I follow, telling:
the road was closed on the mountain
so we climbed on foot through the drifts.
My listener is a deaf ear behind a thick door.
Who has been in love? Who understands
the road and the snow? My listener
cannot see the flakes falling,
swept by the wind, cannot feel
any flurry against the face.
I go on telling
because I must,
it is the only story,
the only one.
On into the difficulty we held hands,
leaping because we could no longer walk,
searching for the correct combo
of tall trees and snowbanks
until we found a place, almost a cathedral.
I am telling no one but myself; I am
alone, searching and finding, wearing
the finest clothing, warm warm warm
while all the rest is cold.

Again I'm Trying to be Cheery

in that way that I do
when I'm inexplicably sad,
a moon on a horizon, sitting
like a dime on the rim of the world.
I try to lift depression, heavy
as age-old rocks; you don't know
about this trying. We've been together
moon-rise after moon-rise
and never have I told you how
something pulls, a weight I don't
talk about, no need to discuss.
One more time I'll let go this horizon--
break away-- it's not so bad--
shrug off this rag of cloud from my face.

Tiny Frogs Fall from the Sky

Somewhere, the news says,
the unexpected come tumbling down,
descending stairs in the air.

Today it's genuine rain on the car
but let me pretend
it's small approvals

too heavy to stay aloft. Surprising
invitations sweep right and left with
the windshield wipers. The road takes

a turn like my coming good fortune.
A pigeon on a wire in the rain
sits, like me, soaking up luck.

In Love With My Life

The snap of the eggshell
against the rim of the bowl.

The sizzle the butter says briefly
to the flat of the skillet. The moan

the water makes as the kettle shuts off.
The smell of bread,

a little too toasted this time, not even
scrapeable. The robin, up to its eyeballs

in grass, stabs the worm; who would
want to swallow the length and twist of that?

How shall I waste
the whole of this day?

Why I Can't Succeed at Sophistication

My sister and I set pins at the bowling alley,
it was mid-afternoon, it was a small town,

never mind where, never mind when.
My parents owned the bowling alley,

all two lanes of it in the basement of the cafe,
which they also owned. My sister and I

would be playing at our cousin's place,
that is, the gas station, and my mother would

trot down close enough to yell that
we were needed, that Adrian wanted to

bowl a few lines. Or she would send Adrian himself
to tell us. We would run up to the cafe, all of one block;

the whole main street was two blocks; I told you
we are not talking sophistication here.

We would set pins by hand, nothing automatic
except the swearing Adrian did when he

bowled a really bad split, say the 7-10.
Adrian was home on leave from the Air Force,

the Air Force because his family didn't have
a farm to give him or a grocery store or whatnot.

Adrian didn't actually swear. I just said that
because I wanted you to think well of me.

Just Now Again I Told My Friend What She Should Do

I told her who to call
and what to say. I didn't
even use *please*, didn't
dress it up as a suggestion,
a choice, a possibility. Do this,
I said. Do it now, I said; tell him
such and such. What happened
to my vow yesterday to quit
instructing others? I am not glad
I do this. Sometimes I deny
I have actually done it. I had hoped
getting older meant wiser, avoiding
stuff you want not to do. But no.
The same slugs inhabit my garden; they
simply have more slime, they are larger,
they are better at climbing the flowers.
Watch that one now undulating up in the world
stem by stem, determined as a bloodhound.
Watch him ingest the last of a fresh pink rose,
slowly waving his ridiculous plump horns.

The Citrus Thief

Again before daylight
she comes in her robe and pajamas,
her slippers soft on the path,
the circle from her flashlight
bobbing on the ground. She shuts off
the light when she nears the tree.
An orange, cold and hard to her fingers,
will twist off to lay in her palm.
It's the stars, closer than they've
ever been, the ancients
who saw them, the woman who
stepped out of her cave, pulling a pelt
around her shoulders. Cold night,
Milky Way, same for any
future bandit, looking up, starstruck,
with a shred of food in her hand.

In the Time of the Great Forgetters

A person could still, by wanting it,
become an animal but you had to
give up words.
You'd still have growling, like the tiger;
you'd still have warble, like the wren.
I wanted to be a snake
and slide into slits in houses,
come up in the spaces
above ceilings or between floors
and flatten there a while
or curl into a circle and wait.
I knew a woman who would
talk to me if I slid out an inch or two
onto her porch. Come on, she'd say,
in or out, she'd say. And I'd choose
out. I'd slide onto the boards
of her porch and rest. She'd remark
on easy things, the heat of the sun
or the phase of the moon. She'd call me
Racer. And when she got tired,
she'd go inside. I'd lift myself
rib by rib and coil up into the chair
she'd left, her body heat still
there in the cushions. I was despised
in those days, like now,
but I found a warm depression,
almost a lap, a little valley that I
fit into. I had given up words,
my soundless tongue flicking in air,
but I take words back again
now and then. I make a trade
so I can tell you this to see
if you forget it or remember.

Insomnia Is a Streetlight

What is there was there
all along. Something can

light it: a tree flailing in a high wind,
a few leaves swirling down,

the predictable flatness of the sidewalk
where no one is standing but could,

if you choose. *Voila!* There's
somebody in a gray parka, shifting

from one foot to the other in the cold,
someone you used to know or fear or love.

There's the smell of hashbrowns
and bacon in his clothing and hair, this

one you used to walk toward, and with
enough light, can still throw your arms around.

And So It's My Birthday, It's Morning

Life, in the form of a mate
who's been up and showered
and brushed his teeth
greets me, who have not,
and tells me he loves me
more than ever. I wasn't ready—
when have I ever been ready?
The stars last night
poking through. The big dipper for instance,
moving slowly, leisurely,
also the bright one overhead, nameless,
inching on in an arc I can only imagine.
So I turn, unready.
Untaught, always
in a different place than I was,
than I shall be.
I open my arms,
I receive.

What Made Diane Rise and Leave the Room

Last week one of the poems
made tears come and it was
too intimate she said. That was the
surprising word she used, *intimate.*
I think it was the line where
you and I look at one another, an ordinary
moment, and then keep going on
this train we could slow
and get off, but we keep on,
and Diane can't, her mate having
died. I wake up and
I want to take your hand,
though yesterday
we had been snarling like dogs.
Let me hold your hand
and look out the window at the passing sky
or scruffy town or scattered cattle in a field,
and talk to you about something, anything.

To My Newborn Self

How they adore you, these two
who gaze into your sleeping face.
How young they are,
her hair dark and full, his back unbent.
Their love will fade, but that is
later. Their love fading
is not your doing.
It gave you being.
You, thingamajig,
sleep. Grow.
Make art. Create like a river rushing,
birds dipping, rising
above your eddies and swirls.
The love that made you
becomes heavy rain upstream, unseen,
keeping your current strong.

Build a Fire on the Ice

Set a pile of sticks burning,
skate around the flames,

shout, laugh,
or stand quiet at the edge, one side

of your face and coat shining
in the light of fire,

the other side a blackness,
your legs and torso warm

enough in flimsy trappings,
though at least half of everything

has no bright proof of existence.
Skim in circles and arcs;

race for a moment
on a crust over untold water.

Our Lives, Familiar

There's a jagged tear
in the kitchen ceiling we stand
under daily, never seeing it.
Under that zigzag
we ask our questions and puzzle out
some answers, take the gloves off,
assess what might come next.
Under that fault line
our guests pause when deciding
on chardonnay or beer. Meanwhile
the powerful go on deciding if
wild spaces, boulders and brush
and bobcat, will remain
or be chewed up for money.
We rein in, we're home again,
talking about dinner, removing
the coat one sleeve at a time
under a torn ceiling, doing what we can
not to waste this one more ordinary day.

Acknowledgments

These selections have previously appeared in the following publications:

Every Last Thing is Transitory - *Bosque*

If I Had Wings at My Shoulders - *Bosque*

He Taught Me to Drive - *Bosque*

I Walk in My House Among Stacks of Papers - *Bosque*

When Wind Blows All Day - *Atlanta Review*

Girl in the Stucco House - *Local News*

Weren't We Beautiful - *Briar Cliff Review*

Occupations of the Body - *Poetry East*

Citrus Thief - *Water-Stone Review*

CPSIA information can be obtained
at www.ICGtesting.com
Printed in the USA
FFHW021951191119
56088344-62142FF